Billy the Bully Goat Learns a Lesson

D0943068

Charlotte Smith

ISBN 978-1-63814-271-3 (Paperback)
ISBN 978-1-63814-272-0 (Digital)

Covenant Books, Inc.
11661 Hwy 707
Murrells Inlet, SC 29576
www.covenantbooks.com

To my grandsons Levi and August

Billy the bully goat lived on eighteen acres of farmland. He was the biggest and meanest buck on the farm. He weighed about 200 pounds. He had a short tail and straight hair. Billy was a handsome goat. He was mostly black with tan and white markings. He had nine-inch-long horns that curved backward. He had a beard that was about four inches long.

Billy stood very proudly. He was stubborn. He could be dangerous. He was the boss. He was macho. He was the alpha male on the farm. He won that title by standing on his hind legs and fighting other males. They would bang their heads together until one gave in. Goats can even be dangerous to their owners if they want to play or if they see competition. They may headbutt you or butt you in the rear end. They can show love, too, with body language or eye contact. Not Billy. He was just plain mean.

There were six females on the farm, too, called does or nannies. They had several babies every spring, called kids. There were other people on the farm too. They were very nice. They were scared of Billy. Sometimes Billy could look sweet until he got mad.

One day Billy was calmly chewing his cud when a baby goat, still slightly unsteady on his feet, accidentally fell and tripped Billy. Billy said, "Hey, kid, get out of my way." Then Billy butted the little fellow.

Frank said, "Billy, don't be mean to the little guy. He's just a baby."
Billy said, "Be quiet, Frank, and get back in the kitchen!"

Mat said, "Billy, we all have to live together, so don't you think it would be better if we were all nice to each other?"

Billy said, "Be quiet, Mat, and get back up to the door!"

John said, "Billy, why does it give you so much happiness to push others around that are weaker than you? You're a strong, good-looking goat. You don't have to do this."

Billy said, "Be quiet, John, and get back in the bathroom!"

Bill said, "Billy, all of us should love each other. We're your family."
Billy said, "Be quiet, Bill, or I will tear you to pieces."

One day, Daffodil, a beautiful brown nanny goat with a big patch of white on her head, accidentally kicked up a little dust in Billy's face.

Billy butted her in the side and said, "Hey, dummy, you better not let that happen again. Stay away from me."

Frank said, "Take it easy, Billy. It's much easier to be nice and forgiving. Everybody makes mistakes."

Billy said, "Go away, meathead, or I'll give you some too."

Mat said, "I told you that you watched too many television shows and played too many video games."

Billy said, "Get back on the porch before I stomp on you."

John said, "All of us would love and respect you more if you were kind and patient."

Billy said, "John, you're just a dumb toilet who lets people sit on you all the time. Go away."

Bill said, "You're already the boss and the oldest goat here. You should set an example for everyone on how we should treat each other." Billy started butting Bill and kicking dust in his face.

Frank said, "Billy, you have everything you could want here—food, a home, friends if you want them. Why are you so angry?" Billy took a bite out of him.

Mat said, "Wouldn't you rather be loved than hated?" Billy started stomping on Mat.

John said, "The best thing ever written was 'Do unto others as you would have them do unto you.'" Billy chased John back into the house.

Bill said, "You're so strong and smart and good-looking. You don't have to do this. Let's be sweet to each other because we all live here together." Billy tore Bill to bits.

One day Billy was angry as usual over nothing and butted the fence so hard that his horns got stuck in the small holes. He tried and tried, but he couldn't get his horns loose. Daffodil, Frank, Mat, and John came running to help him because they were all very sweet. They gently pulled until they were able to get Billy's horns out of the fence.

Billy could not believe they helped him when he had been so mean to them. He said, "Thanks, guys. I'm sorry. I am going to try to be a lot nicer from now on."

"Hooray!" the others yelled.

From that day on, things were a lot better on the farm.

About the Author

Charlotte Smith is a retired high school mathematics and English teacher. She was also a K–12 librarian for many years. She has a BS in mathematics, an M.Ed. in education, and teaching endorsements in English, library science, and administration and supervision. Originally from Memphis, Tennessee, she also taught mathematics in a community college there. She has lived in Santa Fe, New Mexico, since 2005, where she was also a Sylvan Learning Center tutor. Charlotte has published her first book in a series to help people improve their English, entitled *Homophones*.